AMAZING MYSTERIES

WEREWOLVES

BY ASHLEY GISH

CREATIVE EDUCATION • CREATIVE PAPERBACKS

Published by Creative Education and Creative Paperbacks
P.O. Box 227, Mankato, Minnesota 56002
Creative Education and Creative Paperbacks are imprints of
The Creative Company
www.thecreativecompany.us

Design by The Design Lab
Production by Dana Koehler
Art direction by Rita Marshall
Printed in the United States of America

Photographs by Alamy (Chronicle, Ivy Close Images, North Wind Picture Archives, Science History Images), Dreamstime (3duard, Neirfy), iStockphoto (AdrianHillman, chainatp, fitimi), Shutterstock (cynoclub, KeremGogus, Bob Orsillo, RaidenV, Scott Rothstein, Stamatoyoshi, Warpaint)

Table of Contents

Werewolves are shapeshifters. They are people who transform into wolves. The name werewolf comes from a Greek word that means "wolf man." Werewolf stories are more than 2,000 years old.

Like wolves (above), werewolves have sharp teeth and good vision.

There are many types of werewolves. They usually live alone. Most werewolves have fur covering their bodies. They can be black, brown, gray, or white.

Werewolves are typically larger, stronger, and faster than normal wolves.

Many American Indian tribes tell stories of people turning into animals, like wolves.

Long ago, the Greeks believed eating wolf meat could turn someone into a werewolf. Later, people in Europe thought a full moon caused it. Stories from Germany told of people becoming wolves by wearing a wolf **pelt**.

pelt the skin of an animal with the fur, hair, or wool still on it

The seventh son in a family was believed to turn into a luison on the night of a full moon.

Many peoples have stories about shapeshifters. Indonesian **folklore** includes were-tigers. Native American stories tell of deer women and owl people. In Argentina, the luison lives in **cemeteries**. It eats rotting flesh.

cemeteries graveyards; places where dead people are buried

folklore traditional beliefs, stories, or customs that are passed on by word of mouth

During the day, werewolves look like ordinary people. But at night, the creatures show their true form. Some werewolves run on four legs. Others run on two.

Some werewolves may have a humanlike body with a wolf head and paws.

Werewolves are unnaturally powerful as both humans and wolves. They are faster and stronger than average people or wolves. In wolf form, they have sharp teeth and long claws.

Gray wolves can weigh more than 150 pounds (68 kg) and run faster than 30 miles (48.3 km) per hour.

Some werewolves use magic to change their shape. They do not have to wait for a full moon. Many werewolves cannot control when they change. These werewolves may lose control and attack people.

Most werewolves do not keep their human mind when they change shape.

Fewer than 100 cases of hypertrichosis have ever been recorded.

In the 1880s, the Barnum & Bailey Show hired Fedor Jeftichew. He was featured as a real-life wolf man. Long hair covered his entire face. Jeftichew was a normal person with **hypertrichosis**.

hypertrichosis a medical condition that causes excessive hair growth on the entire body

Werewolves are ferocious fighters. Stories say these creatures can live for thousands of years. Only a weapon made from silver can stop them.

Some stories suggest that silver objects burn the creatures.

A Werewolf Story

Once, a father and son stole two wolf pelts. When they put the pelts on, they became wolves for 10 days. During that time, they attacked many people. One night, they fought each other. The father almost killed his son. But a raven brought him a magical leaf. It healed his son. Afterward, the two removed the pelts. They burned them so that no one else would go through what they had.

Read More

de Moraes, Thiago. *Myth Atlas: Maps and Monsters, Heroes and Gods from Twelve Mythological Worlds*. New York: Blueprint Editions, 2019.

Lawrence, Sandra, and Stuart Hill. *The Atlas of Monsters: Mythical Creatures from Around the World*. Philadelphia: Running Press Kids, 2019.

Tieck, Sarah. *Werewolves*. Minneapolis: ABDO, 2016.

Websites

CBC Kids: Seven Spooky Things You Didn't Know about Werewolves
https://www.cbc.ca/kidscbc2/the-feed/monsters-101-all-about-werewolves
Read more interesting facts about werewolves.

Kids.Net.Au: Werewolf
http://encyclopedia.kids.net.au/page/we/Werewolf
Learn more about werewolf history and folklore.

Note: Every effort has been made to ensure that the websites listed above are suitable for children, that they have educational value, and that they contain no inappropriate material. However, because of the nature of the Internet, it is impossible to guarantee that these sites will remain active indefinitely or that their contents will not be altered.

Index